BATMAN AND ROBIN'S TRAINING DAY

MW00876942

Adapted by R. J. Cregg
Illustrated by Patrick Spaziante
Batman created by Bob Kane with Bill Finger

Simon Spotlight
New York London Toronto Sydney New Delhi

SIMON SPOTLIGHT
An imprint of Simon & Schuster Children's Publishing Division
1230 Avenue of the Americas, New York, New York 10020
This Simon Spotlight paperback edition December 2017
All rights reserved, including the right of reproduction in whole or in part in any form.
SIMON SPOTLIGHT and colophon are registered trademarks of Simon & Schuster, Inc.
Manufactured in China 0917 SDI

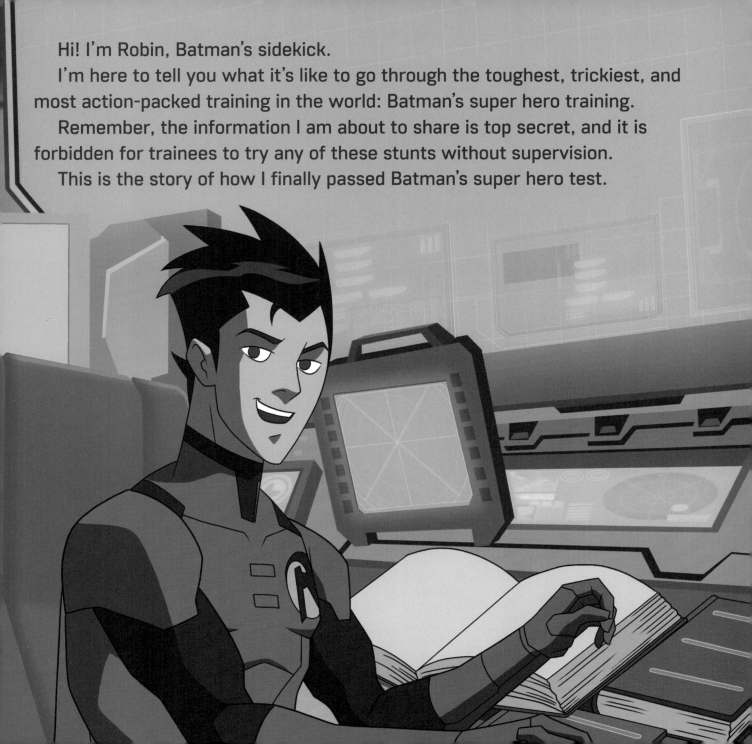

Hi! I'm Robin, Batman's sidekick.

I'm here to tell you what it's like to go through the toughest, trickiest, and most action-packed training in the world: Batman's super hero training.

Remember, the information I am about to share is top secret, and it is forbidden for trainees to try any of these stunts without supervision.

This is the story of how I finally passed Batman's super hero test.

The night began at Arkham Asylum, where Gotham City's biggest bad guys are locked up.

I was helping Batman and Green Arrow stop a jailbreak. The Penguin and Mr. Freeze were trying to spring a bunch of lower-level villains. We had them surrounded when Green Arrow turned toward me.

"Kid, duck!" Green Arrow said, drawing his bow.

I didn't listen. Instead, I turned around and saw Commissioner Gordon standing behind me. "How did you get here so fast, Commissioner?" I asked.

"Robin, get down!" Batman commanded.

Finally I ducked, and Green Arrow shot his arrow directly at the good officer.

To my surprise the Commissioner transformed into a mountain of clay and the arrow whizzed harmlessly through him. I had been tricked by the shape-shifting villain, Clayface! He pushed me down and used the distraction to escape with his buddies.

"It's okay, kid. You're training with him," Green Arrow said, pointing toward Batman. "That's like diving off the deep end . . . of the ocean!"

Back at the Batcave, I was anxious to clean up the mess I had made.

"The key to catching the bad guys is outsmarting them," Batman said.

I knew Mr. Freeze was a scientist, and the escapees had strange mutations that gave them amazing powers. "Mr. Freeze is using the villains for some kind of experiment!" I said. "And the Penguin must be the mastermind!"

"Good work," Batman said.

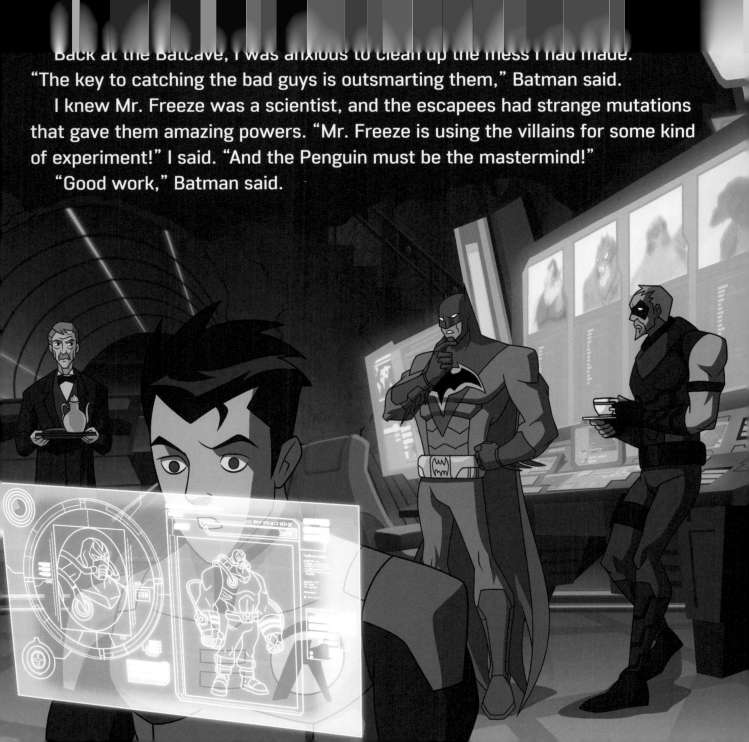

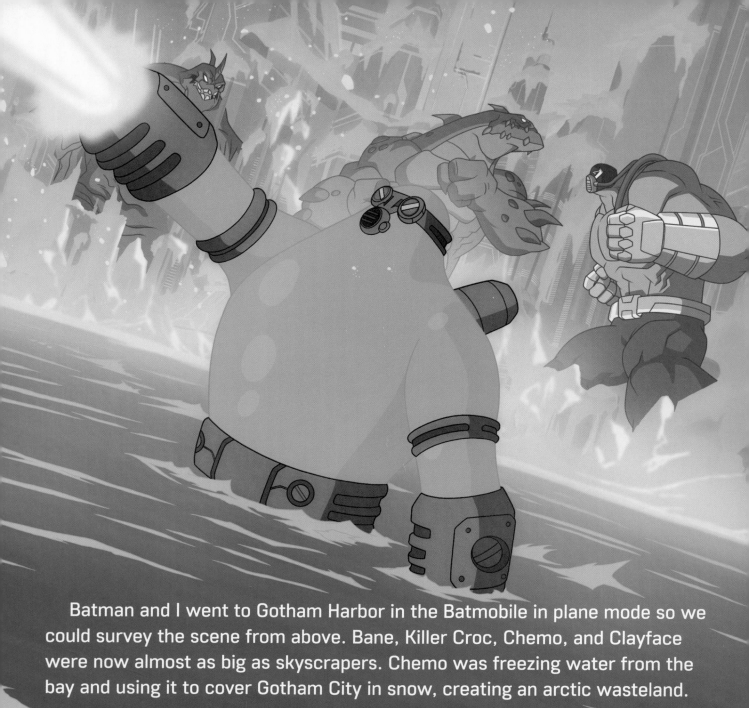

Batman and I went to Gotham Harbor in the Batmobile in plane mode so we could survey the scene from above. Bane, Killer Croc, Chemo, and Clayface were now almost as big as skyscrapers. Chemo was freezing water from the bay and using it to cover Gotham City in snow, creating an arctic wasteland.

Batman landed the Batmobile and took it out of plane mode. "If we stop the mutants, the temperature will go back to normal," he said, tossing me the keys. Then he added, "Keep Clayface from destroying the city until I get back."

Whoa! I thought. *How do I do that all by myself?*

Before I could ask any questions out loud, Batman pressed a button on a remote and the Batcycle roared to the scene. "I know you can do it," he said, and then he hopped onto the Batcycle and drove away!

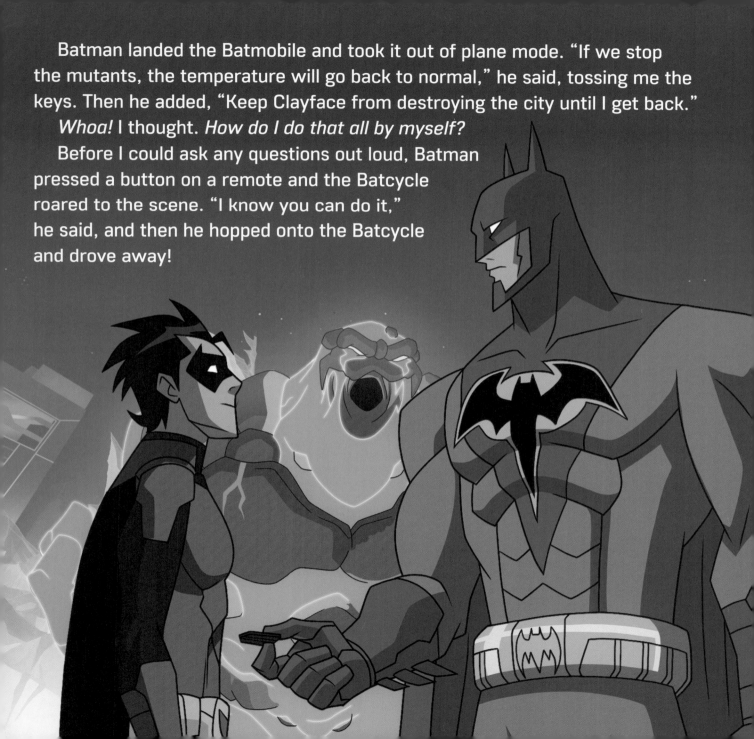

So *this* was what Green Arrow meant about training with Batman being like diving into the deep end of the ocean! I was only a beginner, and Batman had left me alone with giant-size Clayface! I wasn't about to let the boss down.

I jumped into the Batmobile. Once I found the ignition, I revved the engine and stepped on the gas. *Man, this thing is fast!* I thought.

Too fast! Soon I was racing straight toward a skyscraper. I knew I couldn't stop the Batmobile on the slippery ice. *How does Batman initiate plane mode?* I thought.

"Uh, plane mode now!" I said out loud.

Whoosh! The Batmobile extended its wings and soared up the side of the skyscraper.

Clayface spewed burning globs of lava in every direction. I had to weaken him. *What does this do?* I wondered and hit a big red button on the Batmobile console.

Blam, blam, blam! The Batmobile fired a barrage of rockets.

"Eat missiles, Lava Breath!" I said as the rockets exploded in Clayface's gooey core. He gushed lava and started to melt down. I thought I had him beat!

Then Clayface used his shape-shifting abilities to pull himself together again.
"I've got you, Boy Wonder!" Clayface boomed at me. With one blow of his
fist, he knocked me out of the sky.

I switched the Batmobile back into car mode, turning what could have
been a crash landing into a fast landing. Even so, I realized I needed help to stop
Clayface!

That's when I heard the roar of the rocket blasters on the Bat-Mech and Green Arrow Mech! My fellow heroes had brought out their biggest robotic suits!

Green Arrow launched his rockets over the bay. "Let's see what you've got, big guy!" he said to Chemo through the mech's loudspeaker.

"I'll take Bane and Croc," Batman said through his comm. He began to fight two mutants at once!

In this epic battle I had to take out Clayface. I wished I had my own mech suit!

Thankfully, Batman sent his friend Dr. Langstrom to help me. "I have plans for a super laser that could theoretically freeze Clayface in his tracks," he said.

I agreed that this was our best chance at stopping Clayface. "Let's construct it on a nearby roof so we have a clear shot at Lava Breath," I said.

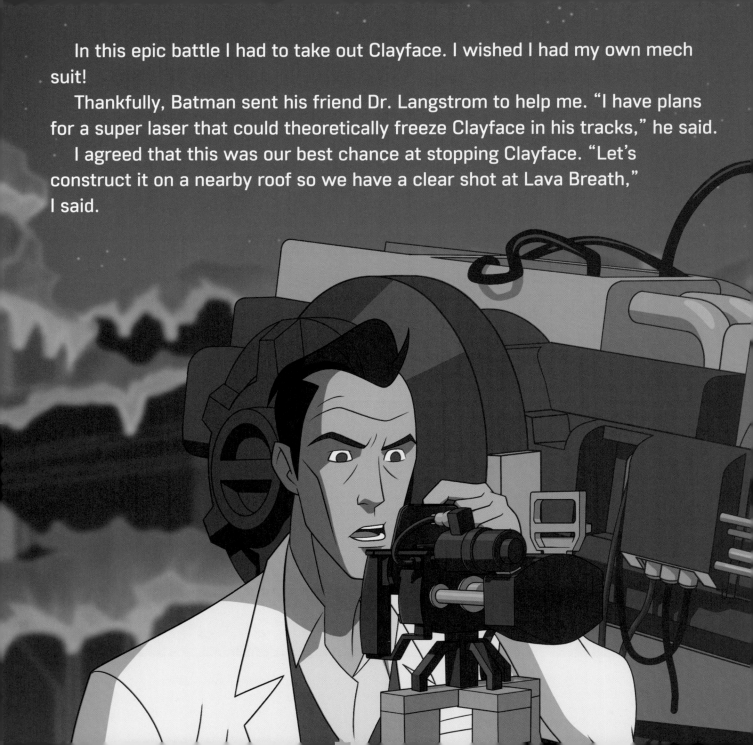

We didn't have long to work before Clayface noticed what we were building. "I'll break your silly little laser," he said, coming toward us.

"Incoming!" I warned Dr. Langstrom.

"I need more time!" Dr. Langstrom replied. The laser hadn't been tested, but Clayface reared back his giant fist, ready to break the laser!

"Fire!" I yelled.

Dr. Langstrom blasted Clayface with an icy ray. Flaming globs of lava exploded out of Clayface as he fought back, but the laser was working!

"Just a few more moments and we'll have him fully encased!"
Dr. Langstrom said.

Finally, the last inches of Clayface froze over, and the mega hothead became a mega ice pop.

"Talk about brain freeze!" I quipped, with my heart still racing, but inside I was relieved. *That was close!* I thought.

Batman and Green Arrow brought in the rest of the bad guys. "They'll be fine once they wake up in a cell in Arkham Asylum," said the real Commissioner Gordon.

"Perhaps in confinement, I might find peace," said Mr. Freeze.

The Penguin was less cooperative. "I'll get free, and then I'll have the last laugh over all of you!" he squawked.

The Gotham City Police began melting Clayface down to apprehend him. "That's my cue to leave!" Green Arrow said to the boss. "I'll see you next time, kid," he saluted me as he took off into the night.

I may not have defeated a villain on my own, but I had made Batman proud.

"Robin, I owe you. The whole city owes you," Batman said. "We couldn't have done it without your help today."

That meant a lot coming from the big guy, and even though he didn't say it, I knew I earned my spot on the team.

Now that you know what it takes to pass Batman's training, what do you think? Could you handle tricky villains, molten monsters, and the most high-tech gear imaginable?

I hope so, because Batman just sent an alert. There's trouble in Gotham City, and he needs our help. Suit up, trainee. It's time to defeat some bad guys!

GOOD NIGHT, GOTHAM CITY

By R. J. Cregg
Illustrated by Patrick Spaziante
Batman created by Bob Kane with Bill Finger

Simon Spotlight
New York   London
Toronto   Sydney
New Delhi

SIMON SPOTLIGHT
An imprint of Simon & Schuster Children's Publishing Division
1230 Avenue of the Americas, New York, New York 10020
This Simon Spotlight paperback edition December 2017
All rights reserved, including the right of reproduction in whole or in part in any form.
SIMON SPOTLIGHT and colophon are registered trademarks of Simon & Schuster, Inc.
Manufactured in China 0917 SDI

It's nighttime in Gotham City, and all is well. The Joker is locked up, and the Bat-Signal is off.

"Okay, Robin," Batman says, "it's time to go home."

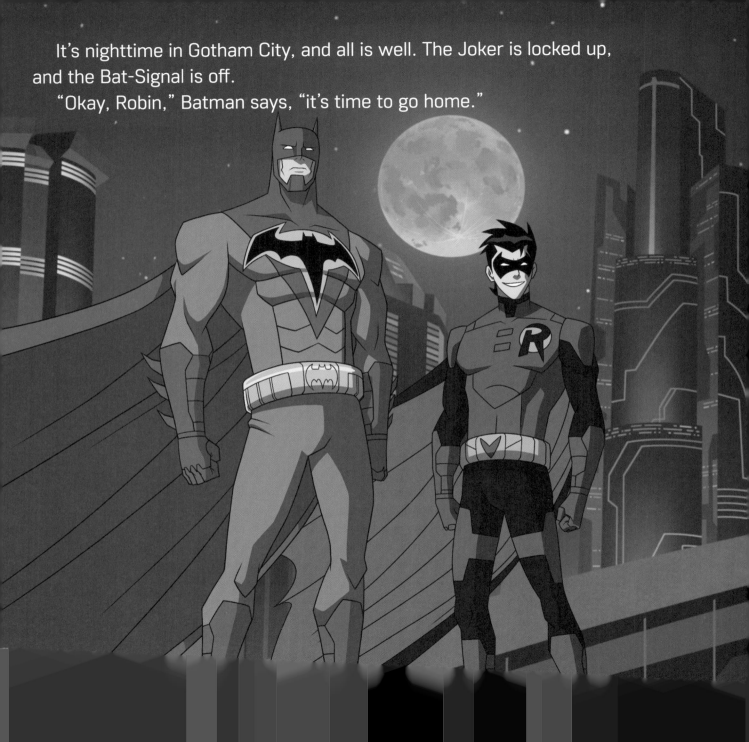

"Since it's a quiet night, could you give me a driving lesson?" Robin asks.

"And risk a broken Batmobile?" Batman says. "Not tonight."

"Then could I take a spin in the Bat-Mech?" Robin asks.

"And risk broken buildings?"
Batman says. "No."

"Well, how about we fly over Gotham City," Robin says. Then he yawns. " Just to make sure there's nothing else we should do_____"

"Okay, you win," Batman says, engaging the Batwing. "But pay attention. I'll show you how I know we're done for the night."

I check on Arkham Asylum. I confirm that the guards are on guard and the inmates are sleeping. Double-check on the Joker; sometimes he is faking."

"Then I fly over Gotham Harbor, where I scan the ocean and sky. Are readings normal? As I suspected, they are."

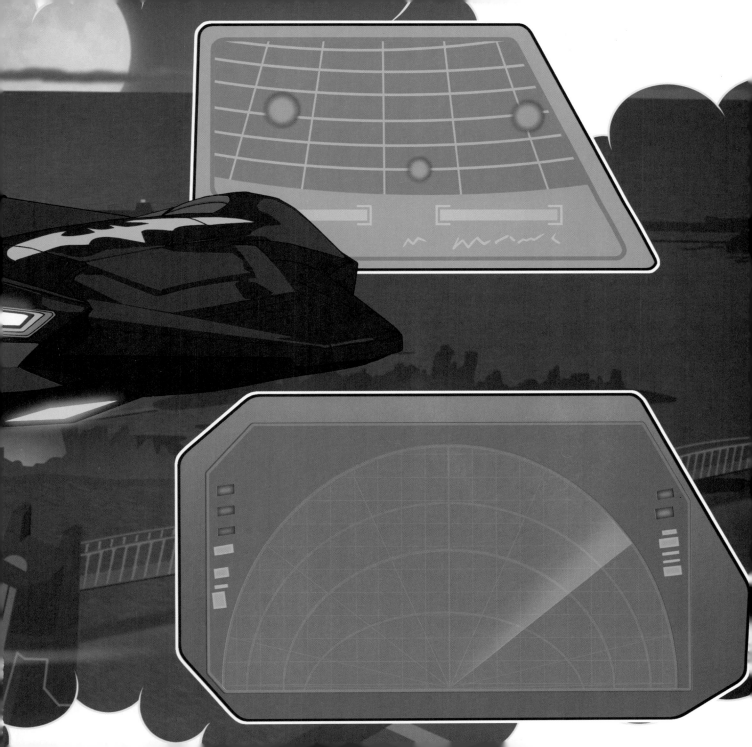

"Lastly, I look at the city from somewhere up high. I see no trouble to stop. There are no battles to win. Thermal readings tell me the citizens are safe in their homes. Our work here is done. Now I should be in bed."

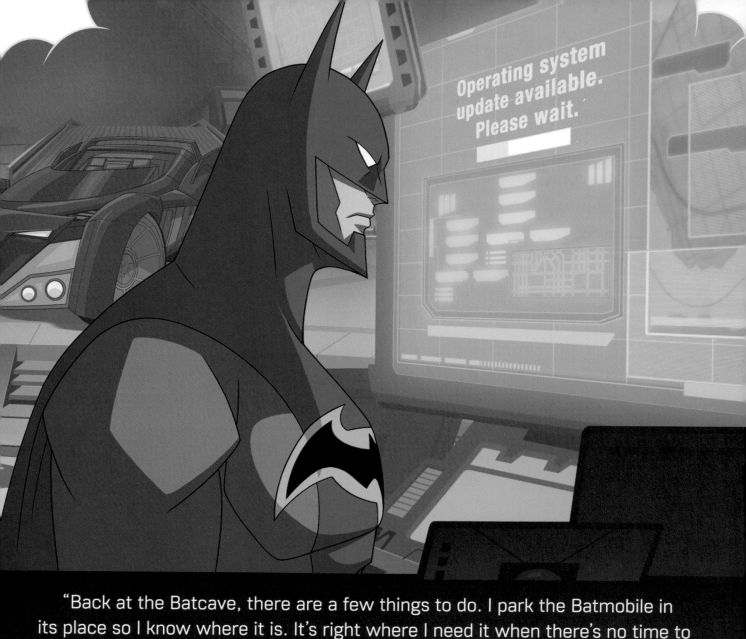

Operating system update available. Please wait.

"Back at the Batcave, there are a few things to do. I park the Batmobile in its place so I know where it is. It's right where I need it when there's no time to waste. I put the Batcomputer in a low-power mode. It saves energy and keeps the system running smooth."

"Then I thank my team for all of their hard work. Robin, you make me very proud . . . ," the boss starts to say, but then everything shakes.

Robin blinks. He rubs his eyes.

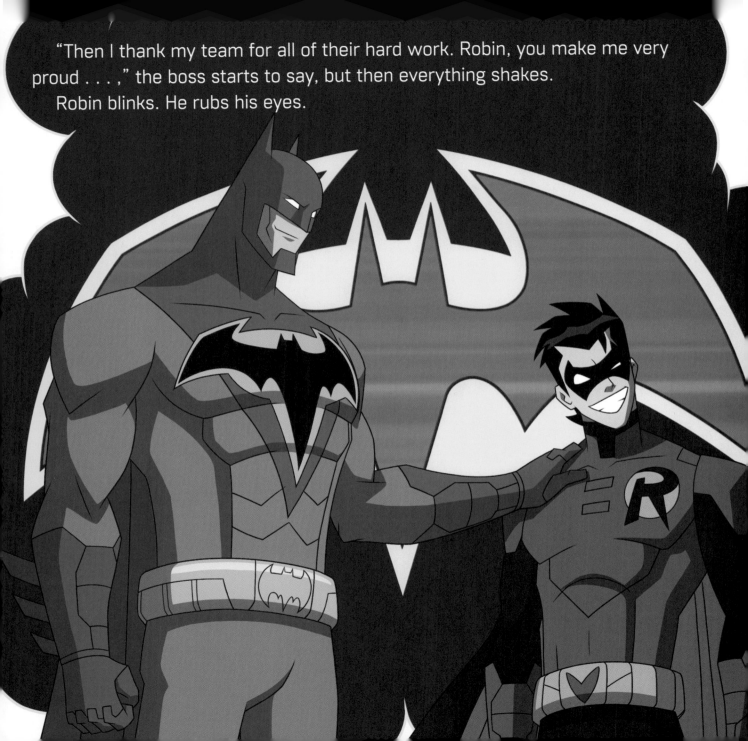

"Wake up, Robin," Batman says. "You fell asleep on the way."

"That can't be true," Robin says. "We saw so many things. We saw Arkham and the harbor. We saw the whole city sleeping."

"You must have been dreaming," Batman says. "Now go to bed. I don't think you realize how tired you are."

"You're right, boss," Robin says. "I will say good night . . ."

"Good night, Joker, you villain. Sleep tight in your cell."

"Good night, Commissioner Gordon. Thanks for keeping watch until dawn."

"Good night, Alfred, my friend.
Thanks for locking the door."

"Good night, Robin," Batman says. "Please get some rest."
Robin nods, waves, and climbs up the stairs.

Soon everyone is asleep—even Batman.
Good night, Gotham City.

GO TO SLEEP LIKE A HERO:

**To wake up ready to save the day,
follow these steps each night.**

☐ Finish the day's work. Lock up the bad guys and make sure the citizens are safe.

☐ Shut down the tech. Put everything in its place. Ready your secret headquarters for tomorrow's action.

☐ Change into your sleeping uniform.

☐ Wash away the day's adventures. Pay special attention to face and teeth.

☐ Choose a book to read. May I suggest a story about super heroes?

☐ Climb, swing, or leap into bed.

☐ Ask yourself important questions:
   What heroic things did I do today?
   How can I be a better hero tomorrow?
   Is my sidekick's birthday soon?

☐ Read your book. Are you getting sleepy yet?

☐ Check the sky for signs of trouble.

☐ Breathe in. Breathe out. Turn off the light. The citizens will need you again soon.

SLEEP WELL, HERO!

(REPRODUCIBLE)

CREATURES OF CRIME

A GUIDE TO THE BAD GUYS

Adapted by Daphne Pendergrass   Illustrated by Patrick Spaziante
Based on the screenplay *Animal Instincts* written by Heath Corson
Batman created by Bob Kane with Bill Finger

Simon Spotlight
New York London Toronto Sydney New Delhi

SIMON SPOTLIGHT

An imprint of Simon & Schuster Children's Publishing Division

1230 Avenue of the Americas, New York, New York 10020

This Simon Spotlight edition December 2017

SIMON SPOTLIGHT and colophon are registered trademarks

of Simon & Schuster, Inc.

Manufactured in China 0917 SDI

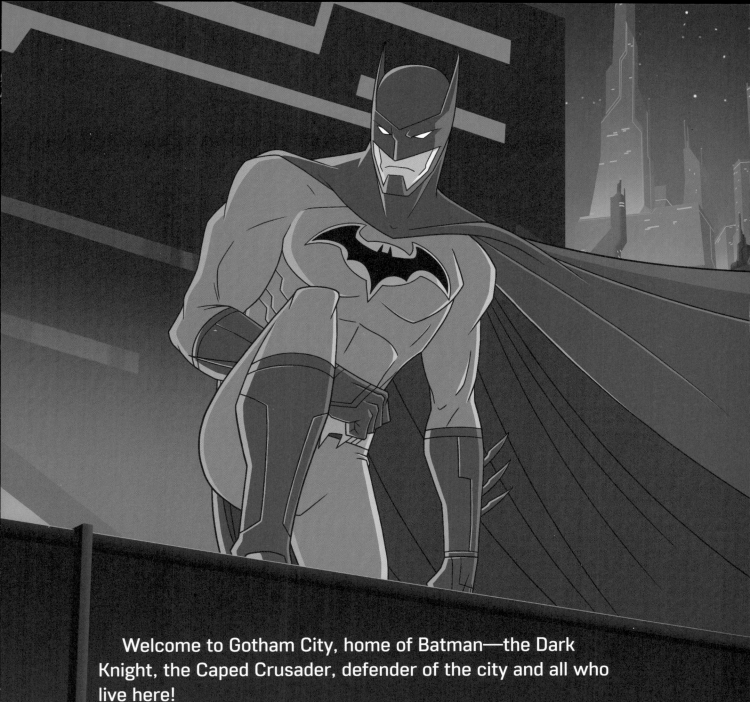

Welcome to Gotham City, home of Batman—the Dark Knight, the Caped Crusader, defender of the city and all who live here!

Batman stops villains—bad guys who are up to no good—but saving the day isn't always about muscle or speed! Batman studies his enemies carefully, using his files on the Batcomputer. With every fight, he learns a little more about a villain's strengths and weaknesses until he discovers how to defeat them!

These are Batman's top secret files on the Animilitia—a wild team of villains led by the Penguin. With high-tech gadgets and amazing animal powers, they seem unstoppable. Can Batman and his friends bag these baddies before they take a bite out of Gotham City?

KILLER CROC

Killer Croc's a monster crook! He is one of Gotham City's most powerful villains; his awesome strength, steel jaw, and thick protective skin make him difficult to beat. Croc lives in the sewer system beneath Gotham City and knows the underworld like the back of his claw. With Croc's help, the Animilitia is able to sneak around Gotham City using the sewers without being seen.

STRENGTHS:
-Armor-like skin
-Steel jaw
-Mega strength
-Sneak attacks

DEFEATED BY:
-Fast moves
-Smart tricks

THE TAKEDOWN:
Killer Croc might be strong, but he isn't very bright. Green Arrow fires a special arrow at Croc. The arrow releases knockout gas that puts Killer Croc down for the count!

Sweet dreams, Croc!

CHEETAH

Don't let this cat out of the bag! Cheetah's powers definitely aren't "kitty" stuff. She has all the abilities her name suggests. With catlike reflexes, razor-sharp claws, and incredible speed, she's almost the *purr*-fect criminal.

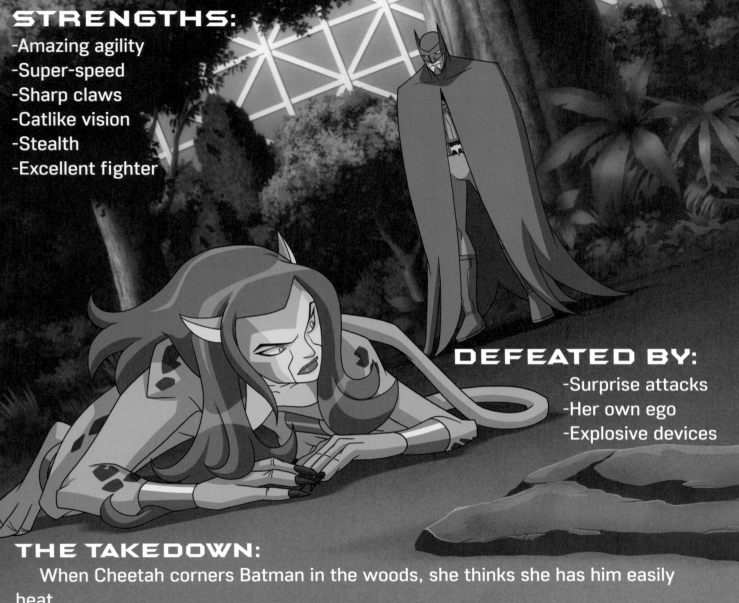

STRENGTHS:
-Amazing agility
-Super-speed
-Sharp claws
-Catlike vision
-Stealth
-Excellent fighter

DEFEATED BY:
-Surprise attacks
-Her own ego
-Explosive devices

THE TAKEDOWN:
   When Cheetah corners Batman in the woods, she thinks she has him easily beat.

   But Batman has a plan: He leads Cheetah on a chase through the treetops, leaving an explosive Batarang along the path. When Cheetah almost catches up, the Batarang explodes, catching her off guard!

   Time to put the cat out!

SILVERBACK

Silverback is king of the concrete jungle. Little is known about this huge, mysterious gorilla with a flair for high-tech gadgets. Secretly a robot, Silverback can communicate with the Penguin's Cyber Animal Army.

STRENGTHS:

- Robot communication
- Internal computer
- Heat sensor
- Twin laser wrist guards
- Fierce strength
- Quick climber
- Gadgets galore
- Smart planning

DEFEATED BY:

- Fast moves
- Surprise attacks
- Short circuiting

THE TAKEDOWN:

Silverback's main weakness is that he loves his plans and sticks to them, no matter what. But when The Flash outsmarts Silverback at the gorilla exhibit, Silverback goes bananas—firing his laser blasters wildly at The Flash. But the Scarlet Speedster is too fast for Silverback!

That's the end of his monkey business!

MAN-BAT

Man-Bat is no joke! He is exactly what he sounds like—a man-size bat—but there's more to him than meets the eye. Beneath his monstrous exterior, he is a scientist named Dr. Kirk Langstrom, transformed by an experiment gone wrong. As Man-Bat, Dr. Langstrom forgets everything about himself and falls under the Penguin's control.

STRENGTHS:

-Bat sonar
-Piercing scream
-Flight
-Steel-snapping claws
-Strength
-Speed
-Sticky bat spit

DEFEATED BY:

-Human emotions
-An antidote that
changes Man-Bat back
to human form

THE TAKEDOWN:

Red Robin thinks Man-Bat will switch sides if he remembers who he really is.
He's right! When Man-Bat sees Red Robin in trouble, Dr. Langstrom breaks free of
the Penguin's control to save his friend. Now Man-Bat can fight alongside Batman
and the other heroes.

Looks like he'll be bat-ting for the good guys from now on!

CYBER WOLF

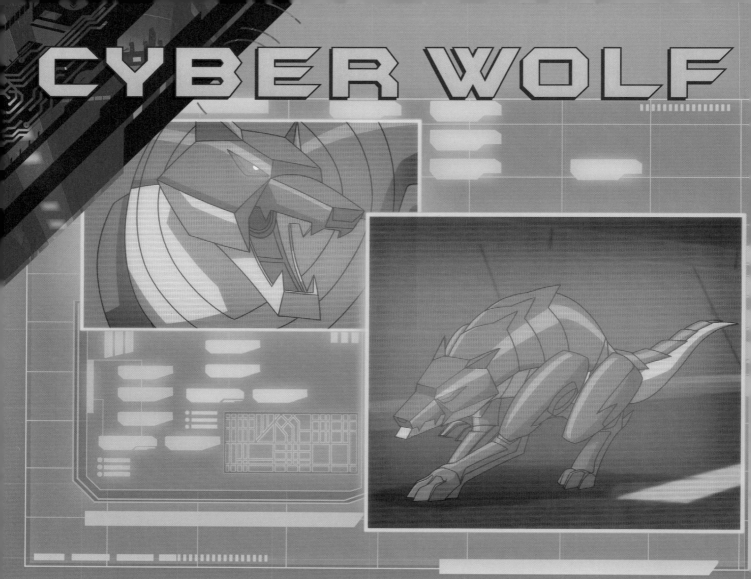

The Cyber Wolves are leaders of the pack! Built by the Penguin to do his dirty work, thousands of Cyber Wolves fill the Penguin's Cyber Animal Army. Each wolf's internal scanner helps it dodge attacks and break into laser-protected vaults. Steel cables in its back and mouth can grapple onto buildings and ledges. A Cyber Wolf can also leap from great heights.

STRENGTHS:
- Superior speed and agility
- Metal-crushing jaws
- Steel grappling wires
- Metal armor
- Internal scanner
- Ability to transform

DEFEATED BY:
- Intense force
- Electrical weapons
- Explosive devices
- Short circuiting
- Reprogramming

THE TAKEDOWN:
Batman and his allies reprogram one of the Penguin's Cyber Wolves to help them fight. The new programming makes Ace a loyal and incredibly strong pet. Ace's tail can be removed to act as a sword, and he can transform into a Wolfcycle quickly.

Now the Penguin will be the one crying wolf.

CYBER TIGER

These tigers will catch you by the tail! The Cyber Tigers have a similar design to the Cyber Wolves, but with a few differences. Cyber Tigers have saber teeth and tails that can rope in enemies. They are the largest of the Cyber Animals, with powerful jaws and mind-blowing speed.

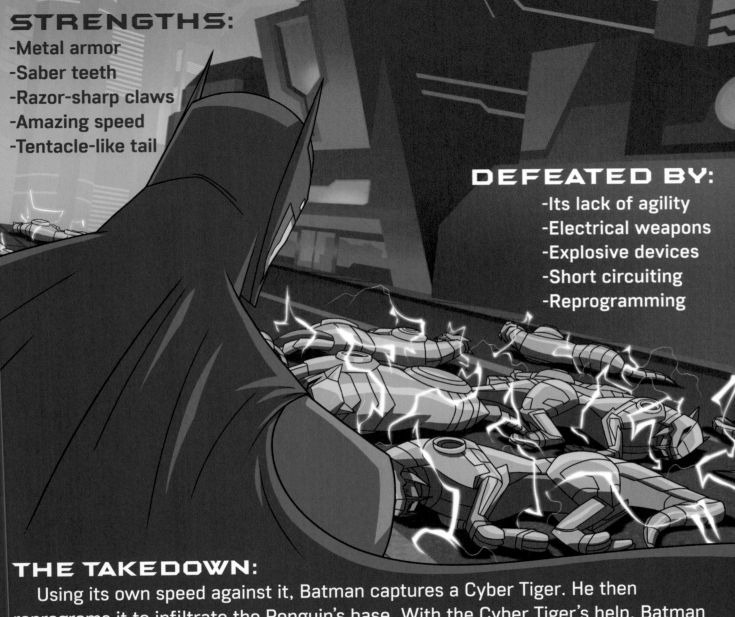

STRENGTHS:
-Metal armor
-Saber teeth
-Razor-sharp claws
-Amazing speed
-Tentacle-like tail

DEFEATED BY:
-Its lack of agility
-Electrical weapons
-Explosive devices
-Short circuiting
-Reprogramming

THE TAKEDOWN:
Using its own speed against it, Batman captures a Cyber Tiger. He then reprograms it to infiltrate the Penguin's base. With the Cyber Tiger's help, Batman and his allies unleash a computer virus that takes out the Penguin's entire Cyber Animal Army!

That's one tiger that can change its stripes.

CYBER BAT

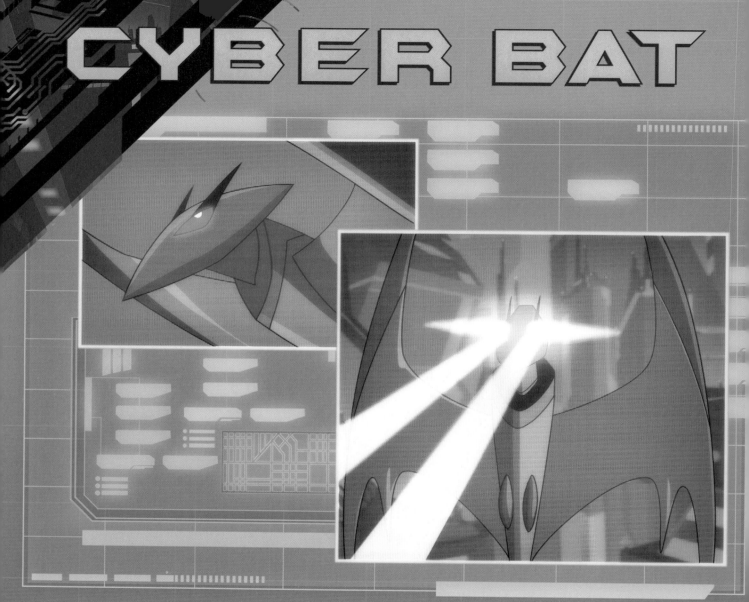

It's Batman. It's Man-Bat! No, it's a Cyber Bat! The smallest of the Cyber Animals is the Cyber Bat, but don't let its size fool you! It still packs quite a punch. This model is the only Cyber Animal that can fly, shoot lasers, and carry heavy cargo while traveling at top speeds.

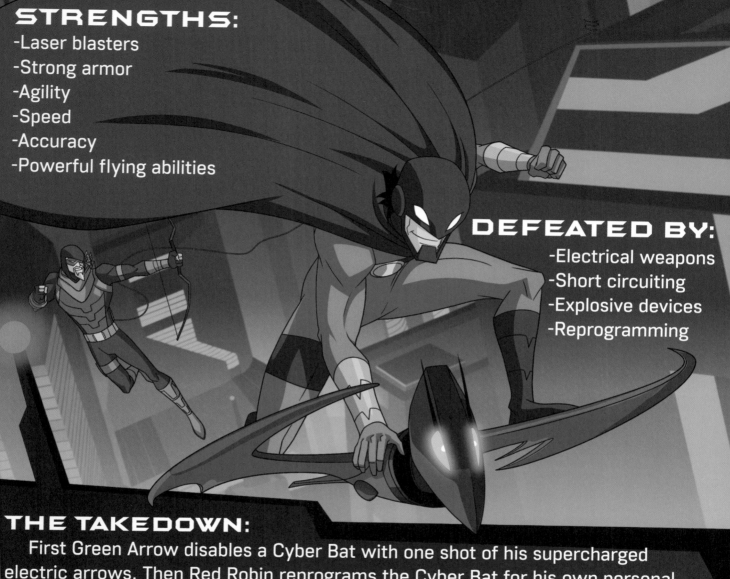

STRENGTHS:
-Laser blasters
-Strong armor
-Agility
-Speed
-Accuracy
-Powerful flying abilities

DEFEATED BY:
-Electrical weapons
-Short circuiting
-Explosive devices
-Reprogramming

THE TAKEDOWN:
First Green Arrow disables a Cyber Bat with one shot of his supercharged electric arrows. Then Red Robin reprograms the Cyber Bat for his own personal use. All heroes need a hoverboard! Quick, strong, and with an excellent defense system, the Cyber Bat makes the perfect vehicle for Red Robin.

Red Robin means it when he says, "Gotta fly!"

THE PENGUIN

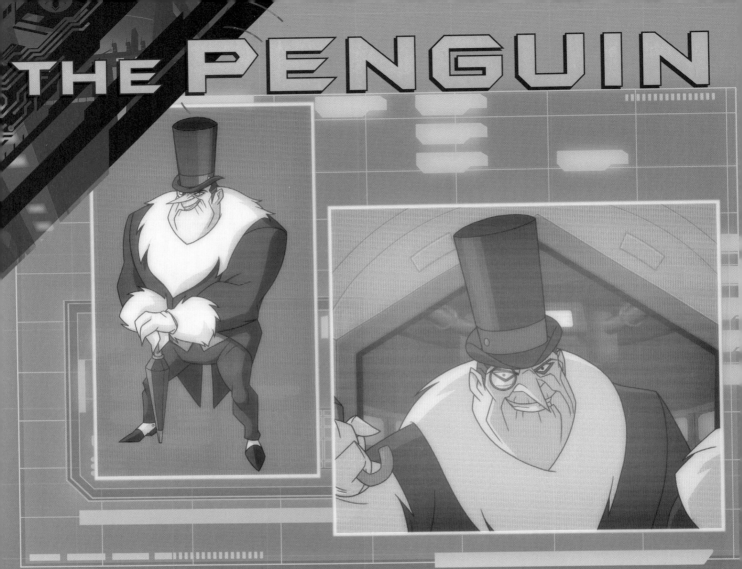

Talk about squawking in the face of danger! The son of wealthy parents, Oswald Cobblepot, aka the Penguin, is the criminal mastermind behind the Animilitia. Though he isn't particularly strong or fast, the Penguin is a fierce foe. He is always one step ahead in his planning and has an army of henchmen to defend him.

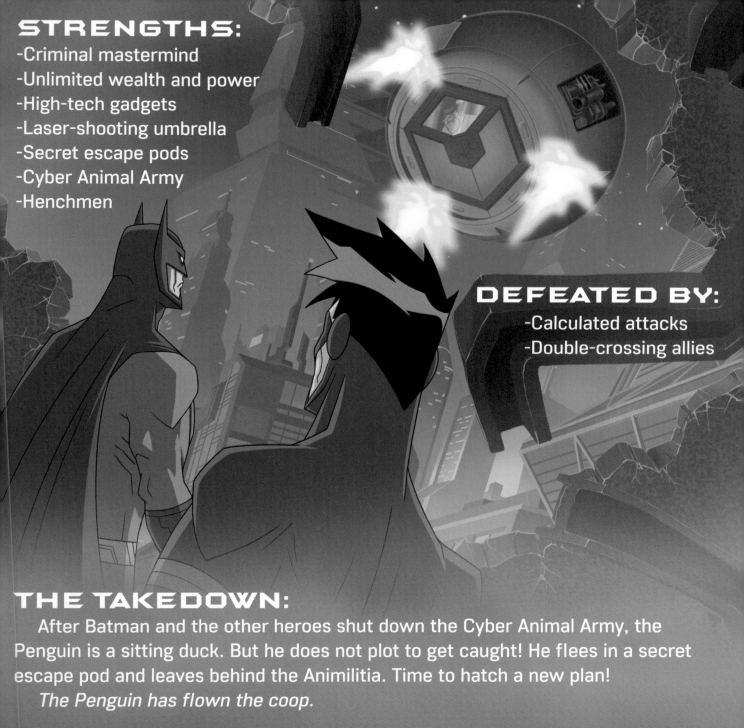

STRENGTHS:

-Criminal mastermind
-Unlimited wealth and power
-High-tech gadgets
-Laser-shooting umbrella
-Secret escape pods
-Cyber Animal Army
-Henchmen

DEFEATED BY:

-Calculated attacks
-Double-crossing allies

THE TAKEDOWN:

After Batman and the other heroes shut down the Cyber Animal Army, the Penguin is a sitting duck. But he does not plot to get caught! He flees in a secret escape pod and leaves behind the Animilitia. Time to hatch a new plan!

The Penguin has flown the coop.

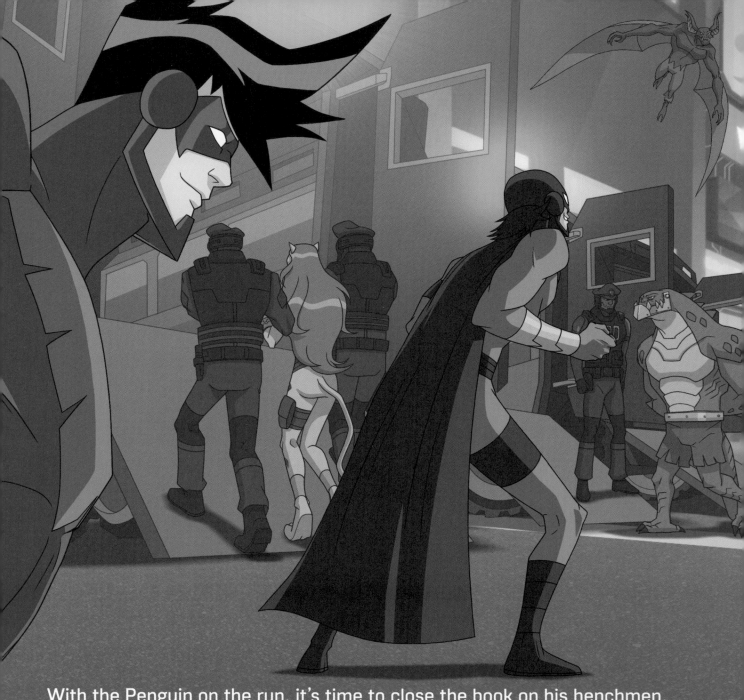

With the Penguin on the run, it's time to close the book on his henchmen.

The Animilitia is no match for Gotham City's smartest heroes!

BATMAN'S TOP SECRET TOOLS
A GUIDE TO THE GADGETS

Adapted by Cala Spinner   Illustrated by Patrick Spaziante
Based on the screenplay *Monster Mayhem* written by Heath Corson
Batman created by Bob Kane with Bill Finger

Simon Spotlight
New York London Toronto Sydney New Delhi

SIMON SPOTLIGHT

An imprint of Simon & Schuster Children's Publishing Division

1230 Avenue of the Americas, New York, New York 10020

This Simon Spotlight paperback edition December 2017
SIMON SPOTLIGHT and colophon are registered trademarks of Simon & Schuster, Inc.

Manufactured in China 0917 SDI

Greetings! My name is Alfred Pennyworth. Welcome to Wayne Manor, home of the brilliant billionaire Bruce Wayne—or, as you might know him, Batman.

Master Wayne has instructed me to give you a tour of the Batcave, his secret headquarters and command center. Are you ready for the tour? Please do come in.

THE BATCAVE

The Batcave is an essential part of hero work, and as such, its location must be kept secret. Aside from Batman's fellow super heroes, myself, and now you, no one knows where it is.

The Batcave has the most advanced security system in the world, complete with high-tech motion sensors and alarms.

THE BATCOMPUTER

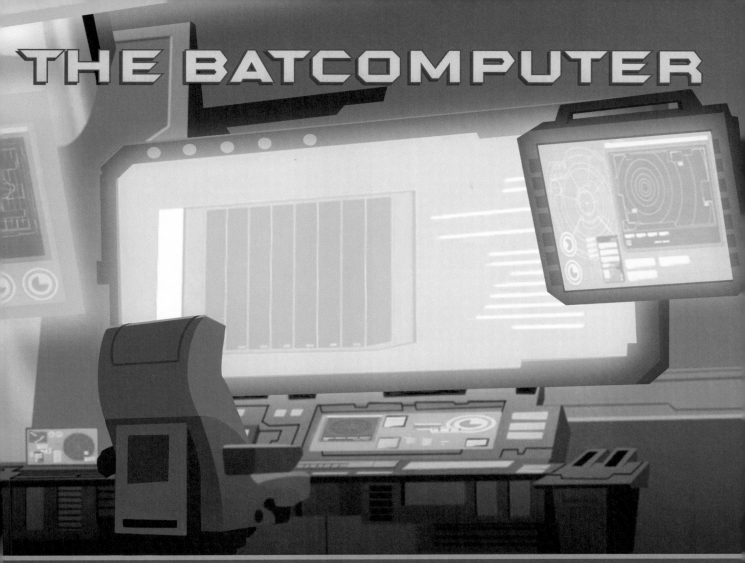

Over here you will find the Batcomputer, specifically made for our Caped Crusader. It is the most highly advanced computer system in Gotham City—and, I daresay, the world.

With its superpowered hard drive, the Batcomputer can analyze data, track crime, synthesize medicines, and keep our heroes knowledgeable about everything going on in Gotham City.

Here you will find armor for Batman and his partner, Red Robin. Sometimes Batman teams up with other heroes too, and you can see images of their armor on the Batcomputer. These high-tech suits both protect our heroes and enhance their special abilities. They also keep their secret identities safe.

BATSUIT

COWL

gives Batman night vision and helps him communicate with other heroes.

CAPE

requires hand-washing by yours truly, Alfred Pennyworth.

RED ROBIN SUIT

BATTLE STAFF

is collapsible, making for easy storage on his belt.

GREEN ARROW SUIT

QUIVER

keeps arrows secure and ready for action.

THE FLASH SUIT

SPECIAL FRICTION-PROOF MATERIAL

can withstand the speed of the Fastest Man Alive.

NIGHTWING SUIT

FLEXIBLE ARMOR

allows Nightwing to use expert acrobatic moves with ease.

CYBORG

Cyborg also fights crime—but unlike the other super heroes, his armor doesn't come off. Cyborg is half man, half machine.

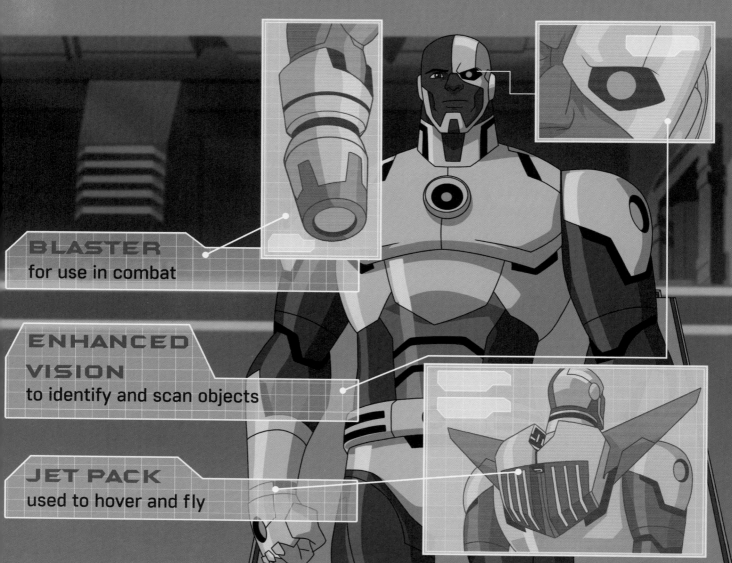

BLASTER
for use in combat

ENHANCED VISION
to identify and scan objects

JET PACK
used to hover and fly

Of course, there are other benefits to being half machine. With the help of his father, Dr. Silas Stone, Cyborg's abilities can be upgraded with new hardware and software, meaning that he can run faster, fly farther, and fight better as his technology is updated.

GREEN ARROW'S ARROWS

On the Batcomputer you will see Green Arrow's massive collection of battle arrows. It takes an expert archer to use these tools.

STANDARD ARROW

A fine titanium arrow with a steel tip.

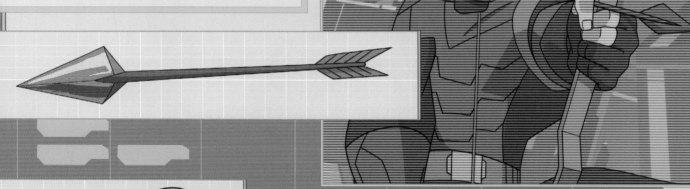

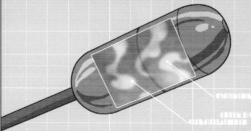

KNOCKOUT GAS ARROW

This arrow defeats opponents with special knockout gas. It can take down multiple super-villains with only one shot!

BOXING GLOVE ARROW

Equipped with a boxing glove, this arrow delivers an extra punch.

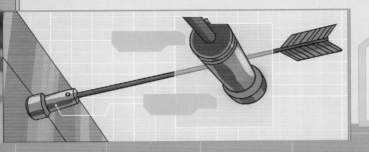

EXPLOSIVE ARROW

An arrow that blows up on contact with a target.

SMOKESCREEN ARROW

When fired, this arrow creates a cloud of smoke that is impossible to see through (patent pending).

GRAPPLE ARROW

This arrow anchors itself to surfaces and buildings, allowing Green Arrow to swing off it, similar to Nightwing's Line Launcher.

UTILITY BELT

BATROPE

UTILITY BELT

BAT SMOKE PELLETS

CLAW

BATARANG (MINI)

One of the most important features of Batman's Batsuit is his Utility Belt. Batman's Utility Belt houses the tools our Dark Knight needs to fight crime—trackers, smoke pellets, lasers, and much more.

Let's take a closer look at the tools inside the Utility Belt, shall we?

STUN DEVICES

Our heroes use Stun Devices to stop criminals and send them running for cover. Efficient and powerful, Stun Devices are useful against Batman's more powerful enemies such as Clayface, Solomon Grundy, and Killer Croc.

BATARANGS

Tucked inside Batman's Utility Belt are his Batarangs. These slim, bat-shaped boomerangs can slice at vehicle tires, electrify a dangerous device, or be programmed to explode on contact. With their many uses, Batarangs are one of the Dark Knight's favorite gadgets.

TRACKER

When Batman needs to keep tabs on a suspicious villain, he uses a special device called a tracker. The tracker sends out a signal that helps our heroes find and catch bad guys.

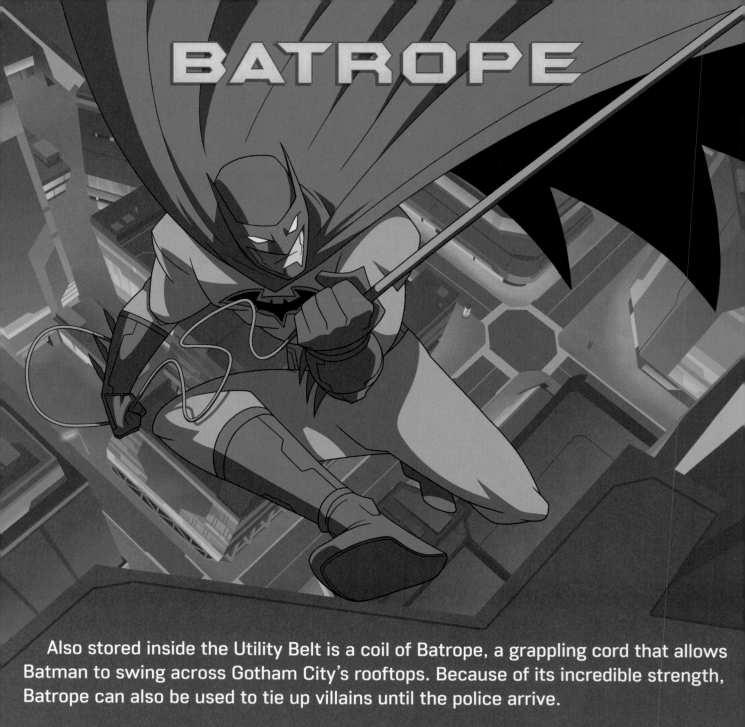

BATROPE

Also stored inside the Utility Belt is a coil of Batrope, a grappling cord that allows Batman to swing across Gotham City's rooftops. Because of its incredible strength, Batrope can also be used to tie up villains until the police arrive.

CLAW

Need to grab something that's out of reach fast? Batman's claw is the perfect tool. This useful object can grab hold of anything—and I do mean *anything*—bad guys included.

NIGHTWING'S TOOLS

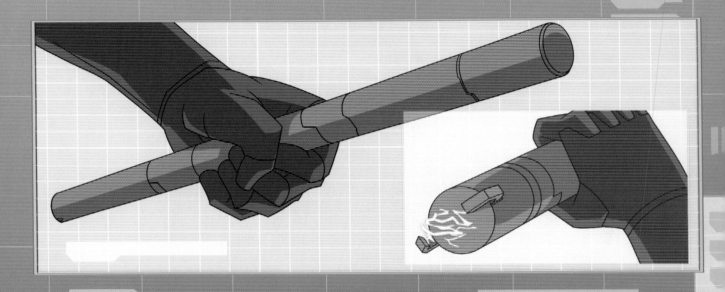

Zzzap! These are Nightwing's eskrima sticks, a pair of electric batons used to defeat enemies. Nightwing can also use his eskrima sticks to damage devices, vehicles, and robots by overloading their circuitry with an electric charge.

To your right, you will see Nightwing's line launcher. As a boy, Nightwing trained to be an acrobat. This specialty training prepared him for life as a super hero, using the Line Launcher to get around Gotham City.

In the center of the Batcave you will find the Training Arena. Master Tim—Red Robin—uses this arena to practice his skills in combat.

Pow! Today, Master Tim is training against two robots. I hope he doesn't hit them too hard; he tends to make quite a mess during combat training.

THE BATMOBILE

Vroom! The Batmobile is Batman's most useful tool. It's a car that powers itself, drives incredibly fast, and provides a perfect way for Gotham City's Dark Knight to get around. It's also very powerful, with two blaster cannons on the front to fire at Batman's enemies.

A secret ramp helps the Batmobile travel to and from the Batcave undetected. This is our newest version of the car, the sleekest and fastest model yet.

THE BATWING

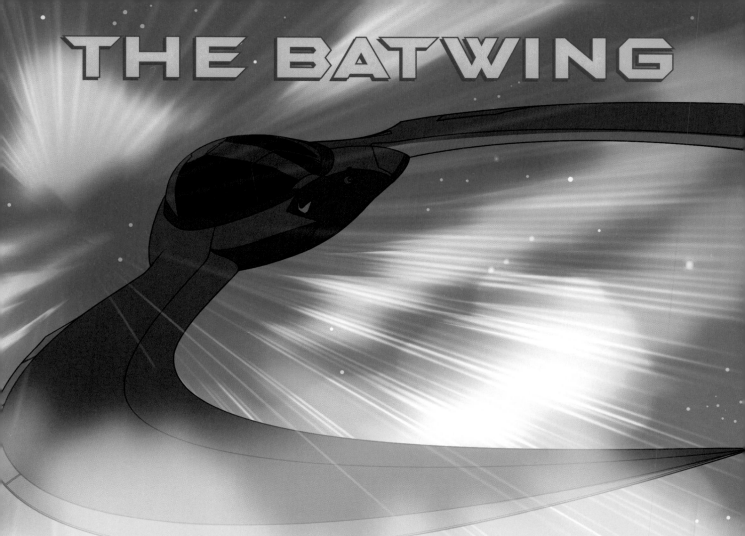

The Batwing is Batman's private plane. It was designed with the most cutting-edge technology and flies swiftly through the night sky. The Batwing also has an autopilot feature, meaning that Batman can summon it from the Batcave with just the push of a button.

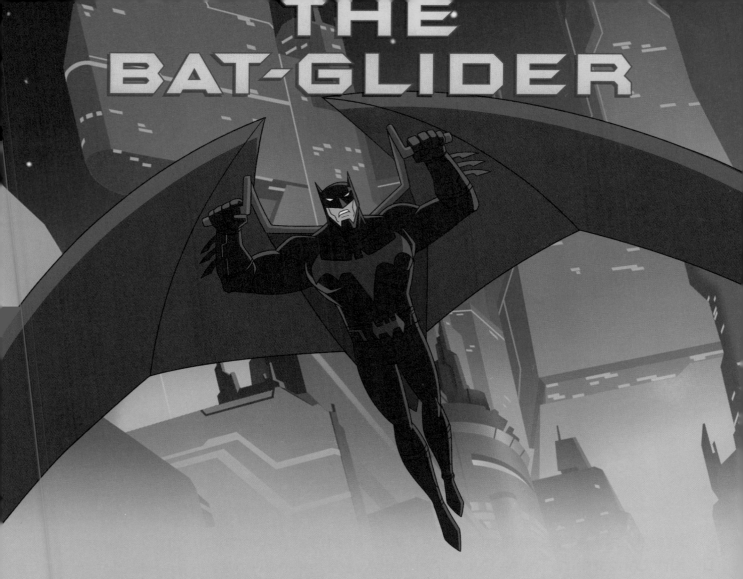

THE BAT-GLIDER

For shorter distances, Batman can fly with the help of his Bat-Glider. Although flight is no simple feat, the Bat-Glider is easy to use—when Batman wants to change direction, he moves his body to the side, and the Bat-Glider follows his command.

CYBER ANIMALS

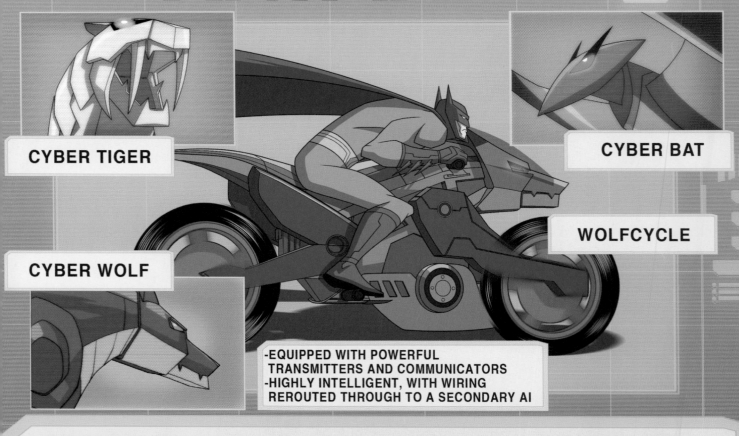

CYBER TIGER

CYBER BAT

WOLFCYCLE

CYBER WOLF

-EQUIPPED WITH POWERFUL
TRANSMITTERS AND COMMUNICATORS
-HIGHLY INTELLIGENT, WITH WIRING
REROUTED THROUGH TO A SECONDARY AI

Straight ahead you will meet the Cyber Animals, powerful robots designed by Dr. Kirk Langstrom. These Cyber Animals were originally part of an evil plot to destroy Gotham City, but Dr. Langstrom helped our heroes rewire them for personal use.

The Cyber Animals excel in combat. Their abilities mimic those of animals in the wild—they can bite, pounce, and jump. The Cyber Animals also have special scanners that allow them to analyze and assess potential threats.

CYBER BAT

can shoot laser beams and becomes a hover board for Red Robin when needed.

ACE THE CYBER WOLF

transforms into the Wolfcycle, a high-speed motorcycle.

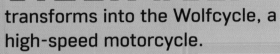

CYBER TIGER

has a tail that can extend and grab onto higher ledges, allowing for a quick escape.

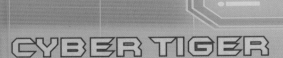

VIRTUAL REALITY GOGGLES AND GLOVES

Video-game designer Gogo Shoto invented this set of virtual reality goggles and gloves. When one wears them, he or she becomes part of a virtual world. Master Tim trains against virtual opponents using the goggles and gloves from time

CYBEREX

I saved one of the best tools for last. Are you ready to be impressed? Here, put on the virtual-reality goggles and meet CybeRex!

Batman used CybeRex to defeat the Joker in a virtual-reality battle. CybeRex is a computerized dinosaur with a blaster on its neck, a massive tail, and a powerful

THE BAT-SIGNAL

I have one final tool to tell you about, one that isn't in the Batcave, but is still important for crime fighting. If you ever need Batman's help, the Bat-Signal is the best way to contact him.

Police Commissioner James Gordon activates the Bat-Signal to get Batman's attention. When Batman sees it, he knows he's needed.

That just about completes our tour of the Batcave. I hope you enjoyed your visit. Do help yourself to some Darjeeling tea and turkey sandwiches on the way out. Please visit again soon, and remember, everything you've seen here is top secret. Batman is counting on you!

THE JOKE'S ON YOU, BATMAN™!

Adapted by R. J. Cregg
Illustrated by Patrick Spaziante
Based on the screenplay *Monster Mayhem* written by Heath Corson
Batman created by Bob Kane with Bill Finger

Simon Spotlight
New York London Toronto Sydney New Delhi

Tonight, Bruce Wayne is at Gotham City's history museum. He has traded his Batsuit for a tuxedo as high society gathers to celebrate a new addition to the museum, the Inca Rose Stone. With the recent crime spree, Bruce and his friends, Cyborg, Dick Grayson, and Oliver Queen, are expecting trouble.

"There are a lot of people who made this amazing discovery happen," says the master of ceremonies. "But Cyborg was the one who actually found the Inca Rose Stone." The crowd applauds the hero. "I also wanted to extend a big thank-you to—"

"Me!" interrupts the Joker as he pushes the man aside. "Howdy, Gotham City! Miss me?"

The crowd gasps at the super-villain. Bruce, Dick, and Oliver slip out of the crowd to change into their super suits.

"I don't want any trouble," the Joker says. "But, my friend here—he *loves* trouble!" With a monstrous roar, one of the museum's dinosaur sculptures comes to life!

The dinosaur turns out to be the infamous shapeshifter Clayface! This is just the kind of trouble Batman was expecting. He and his friends, Nightwing, Green Arrow, and Cyborg, return to the fray and spring into action.

"You're going extinct, lizard breath!" says Cyborg as he fires his lasers at Clayface.

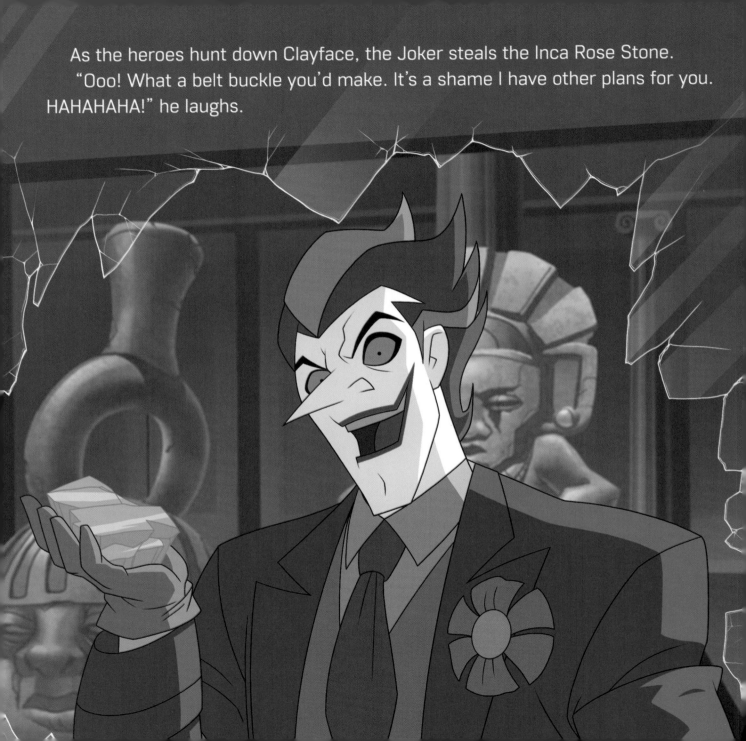

As the heroes hunt down Clayface, the Joker steals the Inca Rose Stone. "Ooo! What a belt buckle you'd make. It's a shame I have other plans for you. HAHAHAHA!" he laughs.

The heroes chase the villains out to the street, but suddenly Batman's Batcycle malfunctions.

"It must be a computer virus," says Batman.

Across town Cyborg's inner computer has also been infected by the Joker's Digital Laughing Virus. As he laughs helplessly, Clayface and the rest of the Joker's gang take him away.

At the Batcave the heroes regroup with Red Robin, just as the Joker's face appears on every screen in the city. "As you can see," says the Joker. "My Digital Laughing Virus has affected every piece of technology . . . which makes me King of Gotham City."

"We're going to have to do this the old-fashioned way," says Batman, coming up with a plan.

Batman breaks into the Joker's headquarters to fight him, but first he overhears the Joker talking to himself.

"It's like Christmas morning, except I'm waiting for world domination!" says the Joker.

He isn't just taking over Gotham City, Batman realizes. *He's going to use the Inca Rose Stone to transmit his virus to the entire world!*

Meanwhile, the other villains are throwing a parade in the street. Nightwing, Green Arrow, and Red Robin get into position to take them down.

Suddenly, Cyborg flies onto the scene. "I'm trying to fight the virus," he says. "But my programming won't let me." As he tries to explain, the Joker's Digital Laughing Virus forces him to fire lasers at his friends.

Inside the Joker's headquarters, Batman finds the virus on the Joker's computer and enters a virtual reality program to destroy it. The virus isn't going down without a fight though: Thousands of virtual Jokers appear in the program, ready to battle. Batman throws a punch at the nearest Joker, but misses.

"It's not going to be that easy," says the Joker's virus. "You're in my world now, and I like things a little crazy."

Luckily Batman knows his way around a computer. He creates a virtual T-rex to battle the virus. With every punch, kick, and laser blast, he infects the virtual Jokers with his own counterprogramming.

"Looks like your virus caught a virus," Batman says.

"Come on! That's cheating," complains the last Joker as it's deleted. "What a way to go!"

On the street the heroes capture the Joker's cronies while computer screens everywhere start lighting up. "I think Batman has beaten the virus back— everything's rebooting!" says Green Arrow.

"I'll be cleaning my hard drive for a week," Cyborg groans as his system restarts.

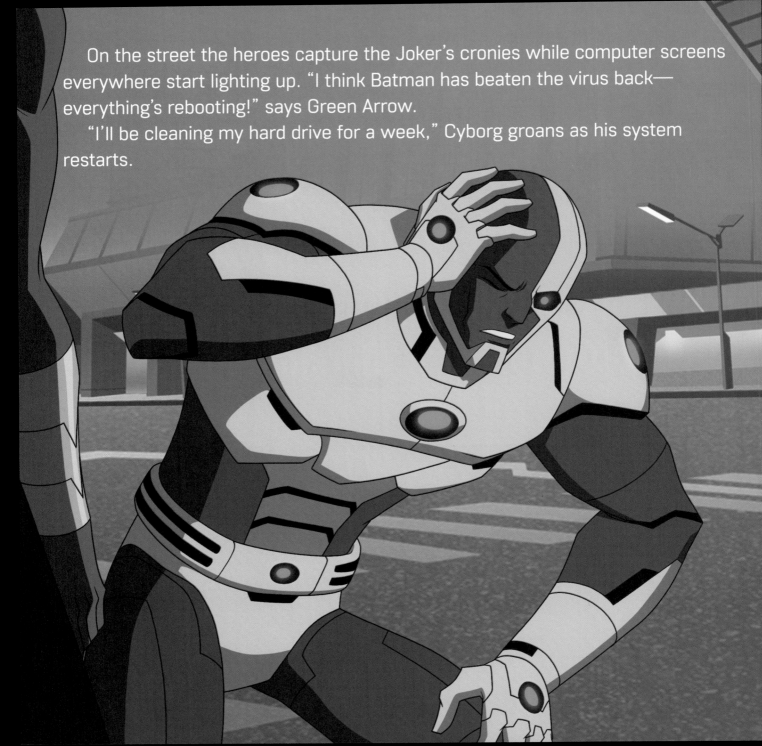

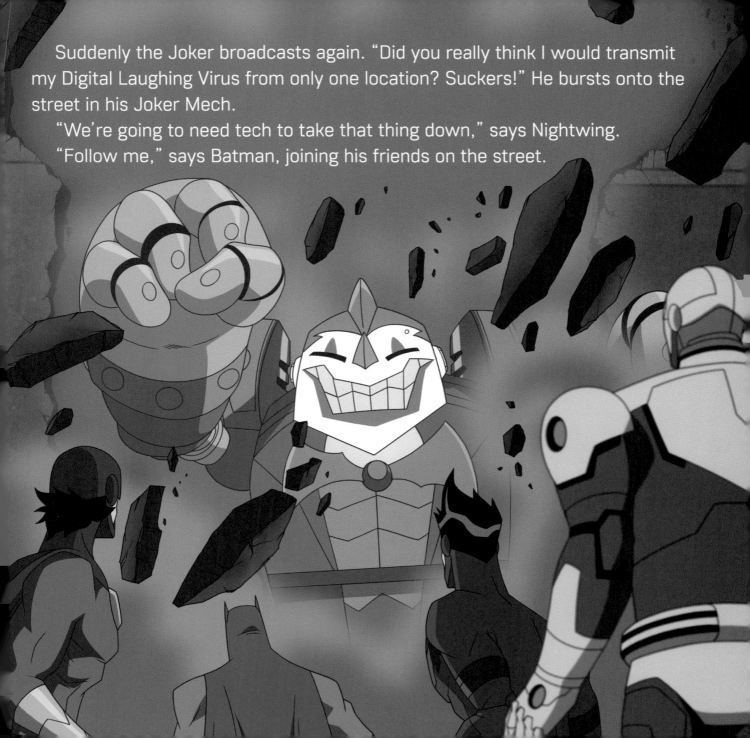

Suddenly the Joker broadcasts again. "Did you really think I would transmit my Digital Laughing Virus from only one location? Suckers!" He bursts onto the street in his Joker Mech.

"We're going to need tech to take that thing down," says Nightwing.

"Follow me," says Batman, joining his friends on the street.

"I never thought I'd say this, but thank goodness for the history museum!" says Red Robin as he and Nightwing speed off on their borrowed World War II motorcycles. Older equipment, like their bikes, doesn't have computers, so the Joker's Digital Laughing Virus didn't affect them!

Green Arrow drives a tank. He brings down the Joker Mech with one shot. *BAM!*

But the Joker escapes again, flying away in his jet-powered stealth suit—he can still unleash his virus on the world!

"The Joker needs a boosted quantum computer to transmit the virus worldwide," Batman says as he trails the villain in an old fighter plane. "The only person with such a computer is—Cyborg!"

Cyborg scans his arm. Batman is right! The Joker put the Inca Rose Stone in Cyborg's arm. With the power generated by the stone, the Joker can use the hero's boosted quantum computer to send his virus anywhere.

FOREIGN OBJECT IDENTIFIED

"You're going to have to attach the stone to the Joker's suit," Batman tells Cyborg. "Attach it to the central core, and that should be enough to overload the suit's central computer and shut down the virus forever."

"Here goes everything!" Cyborg says as he punches the stone directly into the central core of the Joker's stealth suit.

The Joker falls out of the sky and into the river as his suit short-circuits. The city is saved!

"Good night, Gotham City!" says Clayface as he and the Joker's other henchmen are loaded into a police van.

"Quick selfie?" asks a boy, holding up his cell phone.

Now that the danger has passed, the heroes gather on a rooftop. "We combed the bay. No sign of the Joker," says Nightwing.

"He'll be back," says Batman.

"We'll be here when he is," says Green Arrow. "I can always count on Gotham City for a thrill."

On the other side of the river, the Joker walks away dripping wet. "I should be King of the World right now," he says. "Oh well. Maybe I'll open a pizza joint and call it Giggles! Hahahaha! I like the sound of that."

One way or another, the Joker always gets the last laugh.

BATMAN STRIKES BACK

Adapted by R. J. Cregg
Illustrated by Patrick Spaziante
Based on the screenplay written by Heath Corson
Batman created by Bob Kane with Bill Finger

Simon Spotlight
New York London Toronto Sydney New Delhi

Based on the screenplay by Heath Corson
Copyright © 2016 DC Comics.
BATMAN and all related characters and elements © & ™ DC Comics and Warner Bros. Entertainment Inc. (s16)

SIMON SPOTLIGHT
An imprint of Simon & Schuster Children's Publishing Division
1230 Avenue of the Americas, New York, New York 10020
This Simon Spotlight paperback edition December 2017
All rights reserved, including the right of reproduction in whole or in part in any form.
SIMON SPOTLIGHT and colophon are registered trademarks of Simon & Schuster, Inc.
Manufactured in China 0917 SDI

It's a dark night in Gotham City, and high society is flocking to the opening of the Aviary, the city's newest and tallest building. Normally Bruce Wayne would be patrolling the streets as Batman, his super hero secret identity, but this is a special occasion.

"I'll bet you'll get a nice view of the Midas Heart comet when it passes by tomorrow night," Bruce says to the Aviary's owner, Oswald Cobblepot.

"Indeed," Cobblepot says, with a sneer.

Cobblepot takes the stage. "Ladies and gentlemen," he screeches. "Welcome to my little perch at the top of the Aviary. I'm proud to present our company's latest invention—unmanned robotics!" he announces as a robotic tiger, wolf, and bat rise behind him.

Over the applause he can hear a few people laughing at him. "Weird little penguin," someone says.

"That's it!" he shouts. Oswald Cobblepot is not one to be teased. He hits a button on his umbrella and the Cyber Animals come to life, growling and pushing the guests toward the elevator. As Bruce Wayne makes his exit, he's sure he's seen those robots before.

The next day Batman calls a meeting with his fellow super heroes: Green Arrow, Nightwing, Red Robin, and The Flash. Batman knows Cobblepot is up to something. On the Batcomputer, Batman pieces together clues. He discovers the Penguin has been setting up a force field around the Aviary.

"This antenna is built to aim at something," says Green Arrow, pointing to the top of the Aviary.

Batman makes the connection. "The Midas Heart," he says, "Cobblepot is going to crash the comet into Gotham City."

Suddenly, the Penguin's transmitters turn on, activating the force field. A familiar face appears on all the screens in Gotham City.

"Greetings," says the villain. "I am Oswald Cobblepot . . . but you may call me the Penguin!" A crowd gathers to watch the screens. "The Midas Heart is no longer going to whiz past Earth. I have altered its path with my tractor beam. And now I will crash it into Gotham City," he says.

The crowd gasps.

"Don't worry about me," continues the Penguin. "I'll be safely behind my force field, and after you are gone, I will live happily, wealthily . . . and free of you. Good-bye, Gotham City . . . forever."

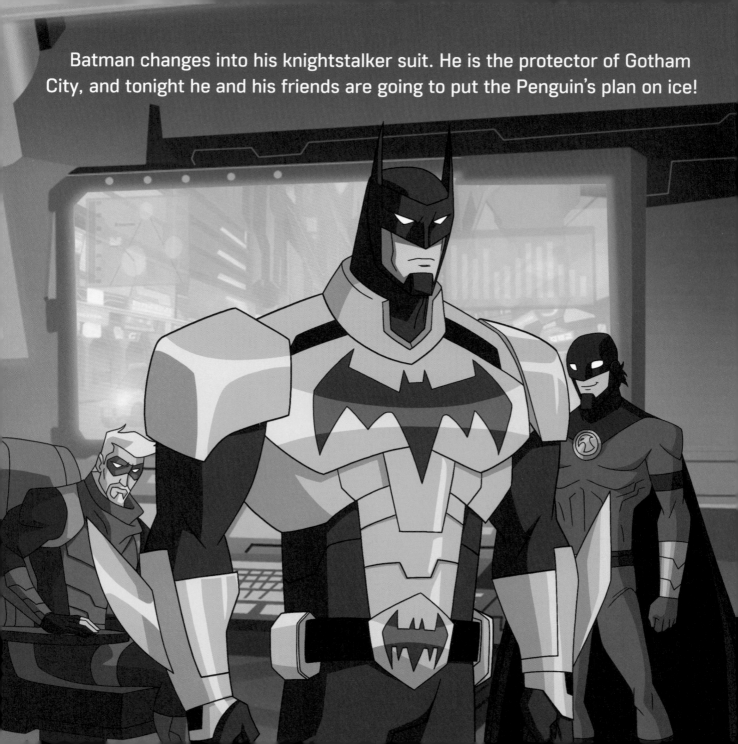

Batman changes into his knightstalker suit. He is the protector of Gotham City, and tonight he and his friends are going to put the Penguin's plan on ice!

In the center of the city, the Gotham City Police Department opens fire on the force field.

"You're going to have to do better than that," the Penguin squawks from inside the Aviary. "This force field was built to withstand a collision with a comet!"

Within seconds Batman arrives in his Batwing.

"Take your best shot, Batman," says the Penguin.

Batman activates his knightstalker suit. It crackles with electricity and surrounds Batman with an amber energy field.

"That's impossible!" screams the Penguin as Batman walks straight through the force field.

Inside the force field Batman takes off his knightstalker suit.
The Penguin's Cyber Animal Army fills the street.

   "Ace, come!" Batman calls. He has hidden one of his own Cyber Wolves in
the Penguin's pack. Ace leaps forward and transforms into a motorcycle.
Batman has taken this Cyber Animal and reprogrammed it to do new tricks.

   "*Fowl* play!" cries the Penguin. "Destroy him, my Cyber Children!"

   "Flash, get that force field down," Batman says through his communicator as
he races off to escape.

With Batman on the run, The Flash zips onto the scene. "You got this," he tells himself. He is wearing a special device that works with his superspeed. The device fires up as he runs faster and faster. Just as he is about to crash into the force field, the device lets him slip through. "I'm in!" he yells.

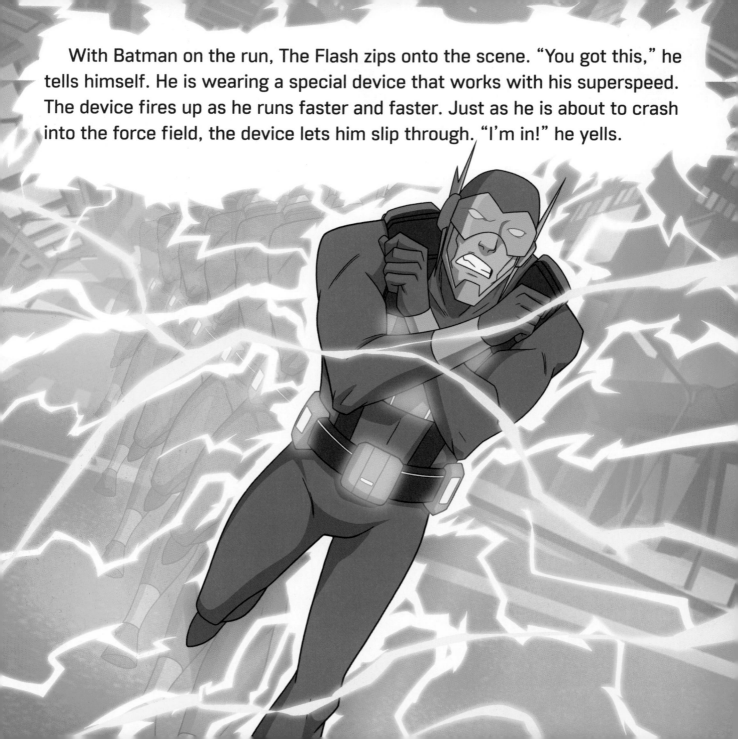

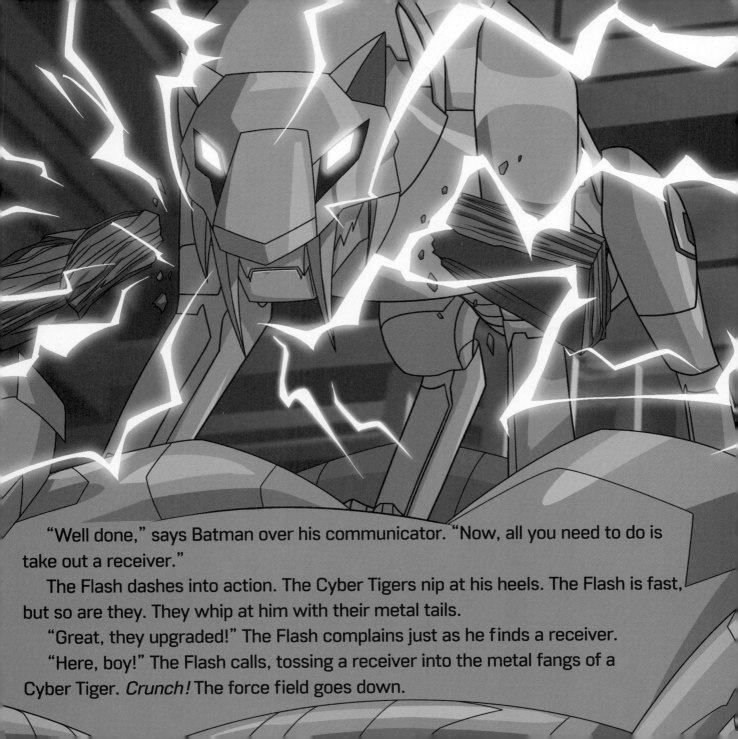

"Well done," says Batman over his communicator. "Now, all you need to do is take out a receiver."

The Flash dashes into action. The Cyber Tigers nip at his heels. The Flash is fast, but so are they. They whip at him with their metal tails.

"Great, they upgraded!" The Flash complains just as he finds a receiver.

"Here, boy!" The Flash calls, tossing a receiver into the metal fangs of a Cyber Tiger. *Crunch!* The force field goes down.

Now Batman's other super hero buddies can join the fight! Nightwing swipes at Cyber Wolves with his electric batons. From the rooftops Green Arrow fires perfect shots. "Don't worry, Bats," he says to Batman. "We've got your back." They take out the Penguin's Cyber Wolves left and right.

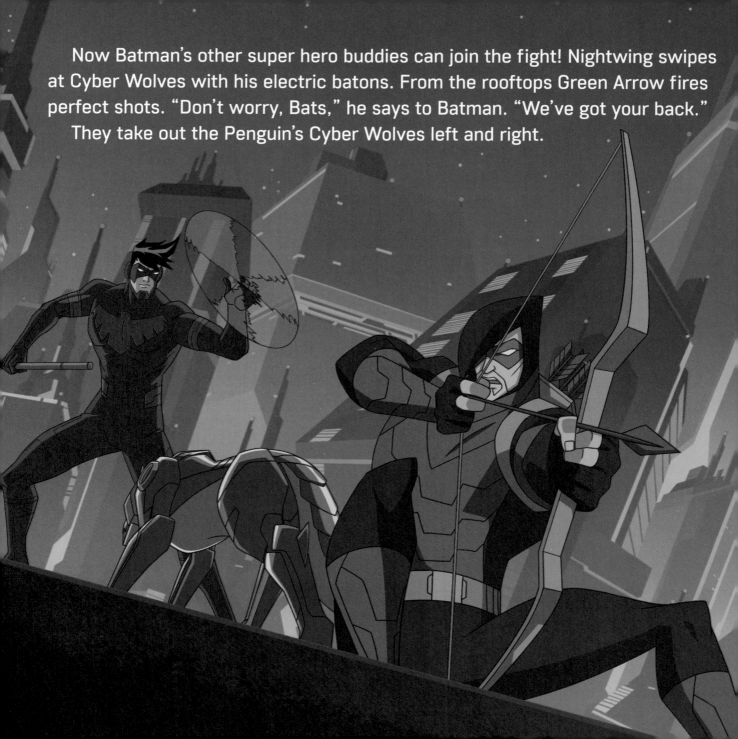

"Well, that's my cue to exit," says the Penguin as he moves toward his escape pod. "I bid you *adieu*," he says to his henchmen just before blasting off into the sky.

"Penguin's getting away!" cries Green Arrow as he fires at the escape pod.

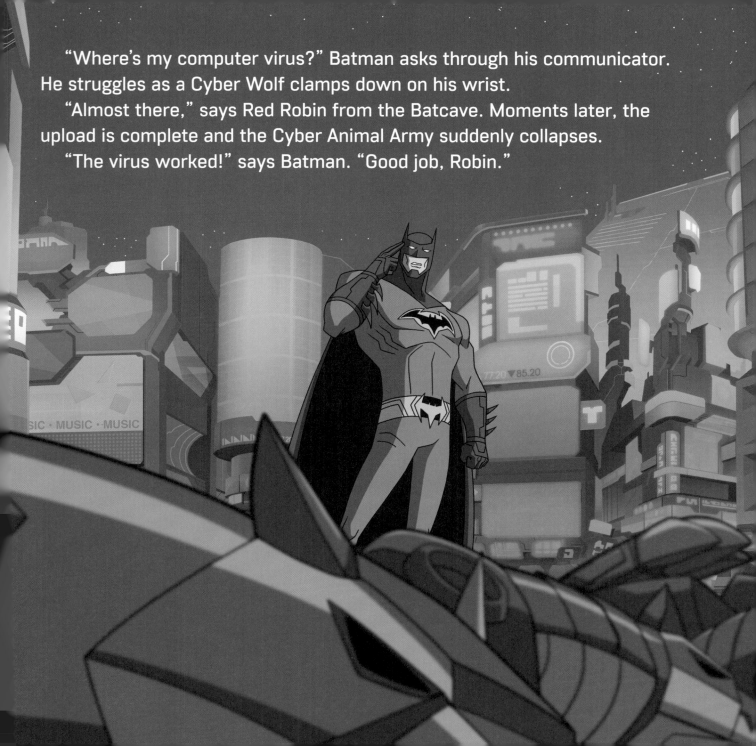

"Where's my computer virus?" Batman asks through his communicator. He struggles as a Cyber Wolf clamps down on his wrist.

"Almost there," says Red Robin from the Batcave. Moments later, the upload is complete and the Cyber Animal Army suddenly collapses.

"The virus worked!" says Batman. "Good job, Robin."

"Now what about the giant flaming rock?" asks Green Arrow. The heroes turn their attention toward the Midas Heart comet, still plummeting toward Gotham City. "Can we reverse the tractor beam?" asks Nightwing.

"I have a better idea," says Batman. "Here's what I need . . ."

Nightwing collects parts for a stronger tractor beam. The Flash moves the force-field receivers to surround the entire city. Green Arrow finds a power source for the controls.

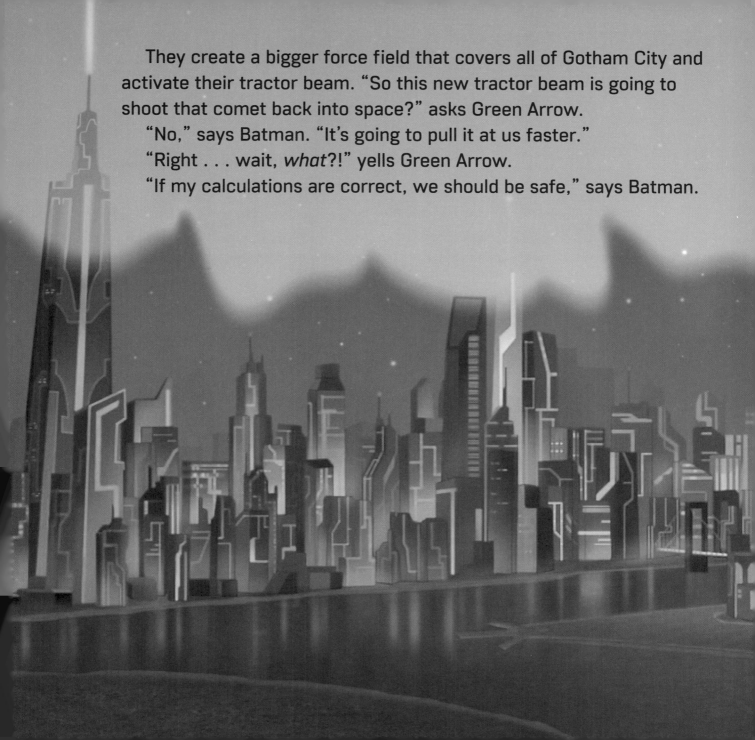

They create a bigger force field that covers all of Gotham City and activate their tractor beam. "So this new tractor beam is going to shoot that comet back into space?" asks Green Arrow.

"No," says Batman. "It's going to pull it at us faster."

"Right . . . wait, *what*?!" yells Green Arrow.

"If my calculations are correct, we should be safe," says Batman.

"Brace for impact. Here it comes!" shouts Green Arrow.

"Oh man, I can't look!" says The Flash as the comet strikes the force field.

Kaboom! The comet explodes into tiny pieces. Chunks of burning rock bounce off of the force field and fall harmlessly into the water.

The people of Gotham City cheer.

The heroes stand proudly and look out over the city they saved. With all their skills, they make a great team.

"It's a shame that Penguin got away," says Green Arrow.

But far away an escape pod crash-lands in the darkness. The Penguin gets out, grumbling to himself. He was supposed to land someplace warm, not here. "Nothing ever works like it's supposed to," he complains.

Thanks to Batman and his friends, the Penguin ended up on ice after all!